THE UNWANTED GUESTS

To my dear friend Gwen lots of love Manos xxx

© Marios Eracleous 2020

All rights reserved. No part of this publication may be reproduced, stored in a retrieval system or transmitted, in any form or by any means, electronic, mechanical, photocopying, recording and/or otherwise without the prior written permission of the publishers. This book may not be lent, resold, hired out or disposed of by way of trade in any form, binding or cover other than that in which it is published without the prior written consent of the publishers.

Marios Eracleous asserts the moral right to be identified as the author of this work.

Printed in Great Britain.

THE UNWANTED GUESTS

MARIOS ERACLEOUS

CHAPTERS

Character Introduction 1

1. Invitation 3

2. The Dinner Party 13

3. Into The Woodland 24

4. The Jolly In The Woods 28

5. Restless 35

6. Missing 41

7. Awakening 47

8. The Calling 52

9. Another Shock 59

10. The Incantation 62

11. The Unwanted Guests 67

12. Judith's Bedside 73

13. The Book Launch 75

About The Author 79

CHARACTER INTRODUCTION

DR EDWARD SAMPSON: Dr Sampson is a demonologist and has a doctorate in History and Science. He is also a curator at the National Museum. He has written many research and historical papers and is now ready to launch his first fiction book at a party. He has invited some close friends to his manor house in a village in Oxfordshire to celebrate the book's release.

LUPIN: Lupin is Edward Sampson's loyal butler and friend. He has helped him with his research and organising appointments. He is harbouring a secret of his own.

LUNA WINTER: Luna Winter is an actress and socialite who has met Edward on many occasions and has been invited to the unveiling of his new book. Not many of the guests warm to her.

DR FABIAN MALONEY: Dr Maloney is a pompous Doctor of Science and Technology. Fabian's obtuse manner infuriates many people but Edward sees past that exterior to a genuine man with a fascinating knowledge about ghosts and ghouls.

DR JUDITH HALE: Dr Hale is a Doctor of Medicine and a Biologist. She is also studying ancient History. Elegant and bold, she has attended Edward's seminars in the past at the museums he curates.

JUSTIN LOCKE: Justin Locke is a journalist who has interviewed Edward and his team numerous times. He is looking forward to spending quality time with Edward and the other guests.

DR JOANNE DEAN: Dr Dean is a forensic pathologist and she also practises in Wicca and the occasional dark arts.

CHAPTER 1
INVITATION

Beady eyes glow in the night,
Howling cries make you shiver with fright,
Feet race through the forest pounding,
Prey on those who tremble with fear
Hear them howl!
Hear them brawl!
Wolves of the night!

It was dark and the rain and thunder did not help the poor soul as he sped along the path. The young male panted, becoming breathless. The sound of stampeding, heavy feet came faster and faster through the deep forest. He stopped and knelt, coughed and spat. He wiped the sweat from his forehead. The young man continued to push himself and he hurried through, though he was slowing down; he had to keep going even though the sound of violent wails closed in on him.

"Nowhere to run!" a menacing voice called out. He stopped and turned around. There was no one.

"You can't hide from me," the voice shouted again. He spun round and still there was no sign of who was talking. "Nobody, nobody runs away from me."

"Where are you?" the man screamed.

"I am everywhere," the voice bellowed and the man, finding the energy from within, began to run again.

Out of nowhere, a creature launched himself at the man as if he was jumping a long jump at the Olympics. The man screamed. His cry echoed through the forest. A claw reached for his neck and the sharp talons of the beast scraped his skin. Blood oozed out. The man tried to escape from the creature's clasp but it gripped his wrists as tightly as if clasping him in iron restraints.

The young man felt the furry body pressing against him.

"Get away from me!" he cried.

The werewolf, gnashing its teeth together, loomed over him. The man tried to back away from the crazed monster but the beast held him in its grasp.

The sudden shot of a gun pierced the air and blood dripped out over the beast. The young man threw the wolf off him and looked at his hand. It was caked in congealing blood. He looked back down at the werewolf; lifeless. He looked up but no one was around.

The werewolf suddenly got up and ran screaming, screaming into the distance, rushing past the menacing trees, tripping over broken branches and stomping in puddles.

The young man remained lying on the ground, wet leaves stuck to his back, his eyes, black as the night sky staring ahead. He smelt the blood caked under his nails, the urge to lick his body overcoming him. He began to change; morphing back to human form, revealing his naked body as he looked up at the full moon.

A howl filled the night sky.

The young man escaped from the dark depths of forest and found himself on the other side of the woodland by a deserted road. He shivered as the howling echoed through the trees. He didn't stop running.

"No," he cried. "No, leave me alone, please."

The beast appeared in front of him and thrust himself onto the man without warning. He fell back and hit the pavement. Blood streamed from the side of his head and as he struggled to set himself free, the beast gripped the young man's wrists again with such force it was as if he had been tied with a rope. This time the creature had his prey trapped and this time it dug his teeth into the terrified man's neck. It drank the oozing blood like it was a sweet wine. The man's piercing screams filled the air.

The beast smelt the man's body all over, from head to foot, and licked the last drop of his blood as it seeped from his neck. It hauled him off the ground and propped him over its shoulder, speeding through the forest's endless labyrinths of ancient trees. The echo of its footsteps pierced the night silence of the forest.

•

It was Friday, a cold winter's evening. Dr Edward Sampson arrived back to his manor house after a long afternoon walk. He did not believe how cold it was and shivered, fighting against the dropping temperatures that chilled him to the core despite being wrapped in his winter layers.

He wiped his feet on the doormat, took off his duffel coat and hung it on the coat stand by the door, then combed them through his hair left long across the top.

Edward, a historian and researcher, had been touring around the world. He was back to unveil his new book, in the presence of all his friends and colleagues, in a spectacular presentation at the weekend. During his escapades he had seen rituals, excavated buried tombs, climbed the highest peaks of mountains and even uncovered treasures from ancient ruins.

Following Edward through the front door was one of his first guests, the movie star Luna Winter. The first of his guests to arrive, she had ventured out with Edward. She pulled off her wet boots and placed them under the coat pegs.

"Edward, that was marvellous. I really enjoyed that and I think once the others are here we should all go for another nice long walk. But it's really cold out there; it's not forecast to snow is it?" She rubbed her arms in an effort to warm up.

"The weather is so unpredictable but I have messaged the others to bring warm clothing," he reassured her.

"I am going to freshen up before they arrive."

Edward took off his boots, popped them to one side next to those of Miss Winter, and slid into his slippers. He walked around the open plan sitting room to the worn but comfortable leather sofas and sat down where he was surrounded by bookcases filled with a collection of leather-bound books, many of them first editions and rare copies. His housekeeper come butler, and most of all, his loyal friend Lupin, strolled in with a tray of coffee; his timing, and service, was impeccable.

"Ah, there you are Edward; I'll just pop the coffee on the table for you. The guests will soon be arriving. That Miss Winter is full of energy," said Lupin as he rolled his eyes.

"She's okay, somewhat eccentric but okay. The others will be arriving soon for sure. Dr Judith Hale, Justin Locke, and Dr Fabian Maloney," Edward said.

"What was it like out there?" asked Lupin.

"Freezing and we're not expecting snow this weekend but I have my doubts." He looked at the rifle that was laid against the door. "Ah, could you lock the rifle away, Lupin? I didn't' mean to leave it out."

"Certainly, Sir," Lupin nodded.

•

It was around 6:30pm and Luna sipped her coffee and giggled like a schoolchild, her dark bobbed hair just hiding her big sliver-hooped earrings.

"There are those who say that werewolves haunt the village. If you listen, you can hear them as their howling accrues on the wind, day and night," Lupin said, grinning at the movie star.

"The sound of wolves coming to get you?" Luna Winter again burst into laughter.

"It's just a legend," said Edward.

"That is correct," Lupin said as he raised his eyes at Edward.

"Folklore," interrupted Edward.

The doorbell rang. Lupin walked over to the door and opened it.

"Ah hello. I'm Dr Fabian Maloney." Lupin stood aside and let him in; Dr Maloney strolled in carrying his satchel and a mini suitcase, and greeted Luna in a rather pompous way. "Your movies are quite something Miss Winter," he said, stroking his full greying beard.

Luna turned her nose up at him. "Well, my agent chooses them."

"We were just talking about old wives' tales, Fabian. Tell me, how do you feel about werewolves?" Edward winked knowingly at Luna.

"Utter nonsense if you ask me," he muttered, putting his bags down and sitting on the sofa.

Edward leaned across towards him, his stockiness filling all the space between them. "Tales like these are scattered throughout history. Every mystery has its riddle and this tale is very curious." Edward ran his finger along the bookshelves to the section housing books about myths and legends.

Dr Maloney took the coffee offered to him by Lupin.

Edward grabbed two books from the shelf, and he handed them to his guests.

"You expect us to believe that there are werewolves?" Luna said as she took one book from Edward. She flicked through the leather-bound book.

"Could be a good bedtime story for you, and think what sort of a movie could be made out of it," interrupted Edward.

"Don't encourage her," called out Dr Maloney.

There was a knock at the door.

"Oh, another guest. Let's see who this is!" said Luna, pushing her fringe out of her eyes.

Edward turned to Lupin who was already opening the front door. There stood a tall male in his forties, balding, and a woman dressed in a tailored suit. She carried a vanity case and a suitcase.

"Ahh, Justin, Judith," Edward smiled and greeted them with open arms. "Everyone this is Dr Judith Hale and Mr Justin Locke, Judith is a lecturer at the London University and Justin is a newspaper reporter," he beamed, introducing them.

"Hello everyone, it's rather nippy out there. One minute it was raining and now it's freezing icicles out there," said Judith, greeting everyone as she passed and taking the cup of coffee proffered by Lupin. "Oh, thank you and it is good to see you again, Lupin," she said.

"You too, Miss Hale," replied Lupin

"Ah, it's good to see you again and hello to everyone else. It really is rather chilly out there, you know, and I'm so glad you have the fire lit." Justin rubbed his hands in front of the crackling fire and held them palm up towards the flames.

"Miss Winter, I heard you were coming along," Justin chuckled.

"Please call me Luna," she winked.

Dr Maloney looked at Judith. "Judith, your papers are joyous to read."

"Oh, thank you," she replied.

"Your most recent one about the Greek Gods gave us quite an insight indeed. Left quite an impression on my colleagues at the university."

"The research is thrilling, don't you think?"

Dr Maloney nodded.

"Once we have finished our coffee you can settle into your rooms and freshen up for dinner," Edward said. "Lupin will show you to your rooms, and we will meet in the dining room at 8:30."

They all nodded and putting down their empty coffee cups, they followed Lupin up the spiral staircase.

Edward pulled back the curtains made up of a heavy red fabric scattered with gold embroidered flowers; flakes of snow were beginning to settle onto the cobbles outside.

•

As the guests spruced up for dinner, Edward unlocked the door to his office. He switched on the light and sat at his cedar desk filled with papers piled high either side of his laptop. He leaned back in his leather desk chair and rubbed his eyes. Moments later, there was a knock at the door.

"Come in, come in."

Lupin entered, shutting the door behind him. "The guests are in their rooms, Sir," he said.

Edward nodded ruffling through piles of papers on his desk. "It's happening, Lupin. I can feel it in my fingers, teeth, and bones. I feel that they are waiting." He picked up a sheet and read out loud from it.

I see them in the evening
Sharp teeth-gnashing
Eyes are gleaming
Blood dripping

"A poem?" Lupin asked.

"Yes, this came to me the other day via email from an unknown source." Edward opened the desk drawer and pulling out pictures from it, he laid out images of victims on the table, one by one.

"So what do you think?" Edward asked.

Lupin picked one up, scanned it, and put it down again.

"There was a horrific struggle here. No human can do that. It's impossible," Edward suggested.

"Then we have a case on our hands but what of the guests? Do they need to be informed?"

Edward shook his head. "No, no, I don't want them to worry about this. I don't know what we're actually dealing with just yet," he sighed.

"But you know, you know this place and its history," replied Lupin.

"Yes and the terrifying things that go with it, Lupin,"

he said. He turned back to the window and, peering through the curtains once more, watched the snow fall to the ground.

•

A mist appeared and the wind became more harrowing, thrashing at tree branches and smashing against the windowpanes. A slither of steely cold filled the study, Edward imagined the guests shivering in their rooms, as the wind screamed like wild animals crying into the night.

The mist broke and a full moon shone bright; momentarily the sky filled with stars like silver bullets.

Out in the freezing cold of night, the beta pack wailed and morphed themselves into wolves, taken over by a demon. They were ready for their kill; the smell of fresh humans enticed them to their prey. They hurried from their sleeping nest and yowled their way through the snow, stomping as they moved together.

CHAPTER 2
THE DINNER PARTY

Luna Winter wandered around her bedroom, listening to classical music to drown out the terrifying wind. She hated the noise, dreading that the night terrors she used to have as a child would come back to haunt her. However, she tried blocking it from her mind and thought instead of the weekend ahead of her. She looked at herself in the mirror by the wardrobe and twirled. She wore a red velvet dress and high heels; her red lipstick matched the shade of her dress exactly... she was ready for an evening of indulgence.

There was a tap at the door.

"Yes," she called out. She switched off the radio by the side of her bed and opened the door to Judith.

"Oh, hello there, darling. Just thought we ladies could go down to the dining hall together. This house is a little too big for my liking. It has an eerie feel to it," Judith said with a nervous twitch.

"Of course. Give me one moment I need to charge my mobile phone. One minute the battery has life and the next it's non-existent. Oh damn," she said, dropping it to the floor.

"Is everything okay?" asked Judith.

"It just gave me an electric shock." She threw the phone onto the bedside table, rubbing her hand on the side of her hip. "Come on, let's go down," she said, clenching and unclenching her fist as they left together.

•

Judith and Luna strode down the long winding staircase. Justin and Edward stood by the entrance of the sitting room and Justin gawped at Luna's red velvet dress flowing in pools around her feet. Edward's eyes lit up as he gazed at Judith's elegant look. Edward popped his wine glass down onto the coffee table. He picked up two full glasses and handed them to each of the ladies as they entered the room.

The soft background music filled the room with a calming ambiance. Luna and Judith stayed close together. All the guests wore evening attire.

"Miss Winter…" Judith pressed her hand on Luna's shoulder. "Have you any new movies coming out?"

"I am on a mini break at the moment but I'm up for a theatre role quite soon, which I am super excited about," she said, sipping a little of her white wine.

"How delightful," said Judith as she took Luna by the hand and carried on observing the artefacts displayed around the dining hall. Dr Maloney rolled his eyes at the socialite.

"Cheer up," Justin said, patting Dr Maloney on the back. "Come on we're here to have a little fun, aren't we?"

"Hmm," Dr Maloney muttered to himself as he glanced at the printed menu card displayed on a table-top easel.

DINNER MENU
Starter
Leek and Potato Soup
Main Course
Gammon with an Orange Glaze
Roasted Vegetables and Yorkshire Pudding
Dessert
Crème Brulé
Cheeseboard Tea/Coffee
(to be served in the sitting room)

Dr Maloney, Justin and Edward stood patiently in the stuffy room that was overfilled with mahogany seating, a coffee table and floor to ceiling bookcases. They chatted away as they sipped sweet rosé wine.

"Rosé is my favourite." Judith inhaled the scent and drank a little.

Lupin paced into the room and clapped. "Everyone, dinner is served." He turned to the side and led everyone out across the hallway and into the dining room.

The guests wandered in, laughing and joking together. Judith's eyes widened with excitement as she looked around and watched the fireplace at the end of the room crackled. "This is so lovely," she said as she nodded her head to the soft music of Beethoven's Seventh Symphony playing smoothly in the background.

The dining room, both long and wide, was domineered by a long cedar table that was set with patterned china plates, silver knives and forks and crystal glasses, which gleamed in the flickering flames of three candelabra. To the side of the table, on a serving station, an ice bucket held two bottles of Chardonnay, their labels visible above the ice.

On either side of the table, the walls displayed paintings of idyllic countryside scenes of families, stags, deer and other forest animals. One of the paintings had a deer just staring out into the forest clearing where it was surrounded by autumnal leaves. Another piece of art showed an idyllic country house and a family playing cricket on the manicured lawn on a bright summer's day.

Edward unbuttoned his dinner jacket, revealing a black shirt and blue cummerbund across his waist, and pulled out the seat next to him for Judith. Judith sat down and Justin did the same for Luna. He was still eyeing her like a lovesick teenager. Dr Maloney sat at the other end of the table, a sheen of sweat appearing across his balding head.

Lupin, wearing a purple shirt and brocaded waistcoat in the same shade and black trousers, wheeled the hostess trolley in. A stainless steel soup tureen with a matching ladle poised by its side dominated the mobile unit. The smell of the creamy leek and potato soup filled the air as Lupin took off the bowl's cover with an exaggerated sweep of his arm.

Lupin served the starter, serving the ladies first.

Justin piped up. "Tell me, Doctor Sampson. There has been talk of ghostly goings-on in these parts of the village. Can you tell me if this is true or not?"

There was giggling from Judith, and natter from Dr

Maloney and Luna. "You shouldn't be reporting on anything that isn't true." His butler looked at him.

"This house quite interests me," interrupted Judith and she smiled as Lupin handed her a bowl of soup. "There are many staircases and rooms, I haven't explored yet."

"The rooms in this house are extraordinary but I have not managed to explore them since arriving," replied Edward, sipping a little of his wine. "Even though the house has been in the family for centuries, there are parts of it I don't remember or even recall ever visiting."

"So when did you arrive here?" asked Justin.

"I came only a matter of three months ago. Judith was lucky to be the first to visit as she was passing by the first weekend when I moved in. I was on tour and found out I'd inherited this place from my great aunt Genevieve. I do of course remember coming here as a child but I have not yet been able to explore fully," he added.

"Lupin must be a great asset here, doing everything," she said.

"He's a great asset yes and I'm so happy he's here. He does everything including the cooking and cleaning for me."

"To say the least it will be fun exploring," said Judith

"Here, here," Luna said. "The indoors and outdoors too. The woodland is the most wondrous place and I think we should have a jolly there tomorrow." She touched Edward's arm. "What do you say, Edward?"

They all agreed.

"Okay, you twisted my arm," he laughed. "Come on, everyone, tuck in before the soup goes cold."

Within minutes, the main course was served, gammon covered in a glaze of orange and peppers, Yorkshire puddings, and roasted carrots and parsnips. Everyone seemed to enjoy the food. The food smell intensified as Lupin poured gravy over the gammon. Justin licked his lips with delight as he began to tuck in.

Judith inhaled the wondrous fragrance of the orange as she cut into a slice of gammon, the juice filling her mouth. She drank a little of her bubbly Chardonnay. "Gorgeous," she said smiling. The light of the candelabra highlighted her silver grey hair.

Luna breathed in the sweet glazed gammon. "I must get this recipe," she said.

•

After dinner, the party moved into the sitting room where the cheeseboard, coffee, and tea were laid out.

Luna watched snowflakes fall to the ground. "Oh, I love it when it snows," she said, peering through the window. "You know, I fancy a cigarette. Anyone want to join me?"

"I'll come with you," said Justin. "I'll want to interview you as well for the entertainment page. Find out what you're going to be up to in your career," he said.

"Very well… if you must." She turned her nose up.

"It gets rather cold out there so wrap up warm and be careful," interrupted Edward. Luna nodded and she and Justin grabbed their coats and headed outside.

"He's right you know it is cold," Luna shivered and got out a cigarette and a lighter.

"Yes, the snow's become quite heavy and yet you want to go out into the woods tomorrow," he replied.

"It will give us something to do," she giggled.

"Yeah but look at it," he said, bemused.

"Mr. Locke, could I ask you a question?" she asked.

"Go on," he said.

But before she could ask her question, Luna noticed the stony ground as she exhaled the cigarette smoke. She scanned the area, shocked to witness a trickle of dark red running like a stream close to her feet. It was blood. She screamed.

•

The party continued inside the house. Judith tilted her head towards the window. "Oh my goodness, that sounded like Luna." She stood up rushing over.

Edward stopped what he was doing and looked at his worried guests.

"It's Luna. It's definitely her," replied Edward. He jumped from his seat, and rushed outside. The others followed.

"Luna, Luna, what's wrong?" Edward asked as he approached, puffing from the sprint so soon after their meal.

Luna pointed to the floor.

"There's blood everywhere," she screamed again, dropping her cigarette, with its smudge of her red lipstick around it, to the ground.

Edward followed the blood, which trailed the ten metres or so from Luna's feet to the entrance of the driveway.

"What on earth?" he mumbled to himself.

Judith gasped as she looked at the blood sprawled along the ground. She took Luna in her arms and cradled her. "Oh you poor girl, are you okay?"

"Just a little shaken, that's all," she replied.

"Why is there blood everywhere?" Dr Maloney boomed.

"Everyone back into the house," shouted Edward.

Everybody rushed back inside as Judith and Justin helped Luna indoors.

Edward stumbled inside after his guests, locking and bolting the doors behind him.

•

A wolf man lurked above the roof and snarled as he scraped his claws along the tiles. He closed his eyes and howled against the moon as the snow fell upon his muscular back and clung to his fur.

•

"Was that blood, Mr Sampson?" called Lupin, his bushy black eyebrows furrowing in question.

Justin trembled. "I think it was," he replied.

"Well there might be a murderer on the loose," shouted Dr Maloney, tugging at his beard. "Or worse," he continued as he grabbed his drink and finished it all in one go.

"Just calm down," Edward reassured everyone.

"What should we do then?" boomed Justin.

"I think we need a nightcap and I will tell the officials tomorrow… for all we know the blood Luna and Justin saw could be that of an animal," Edward said.

"The wolves have arrived," Judith commented, her face paling in horror.

"I doubt any wolves would come this close to the house, Miss Hale," Justin replied.

"I think it's time for us to all go to bed and figure this out in the morning," said Edward.

"I don't think that I'll be in the right mind to sleep by myself tonight," Luna said still shaken up.

"It's okay I will share with you," Judith replied. "I will be up shortly."

•

Everyone headed to bed. Judith sat on the sofa as Edward began tidying up. "Oh leave that for Lupin," she said, patting the seat next to her so that he could join her.

"Are you nervous?"

"About the presentation?" He nodded. "I'm used to giving tours, making press release statements and heading up meetings. Yet, you're my friends and somehow that makes me more nervous," he added.

"We all get nervous. I'm nervous sitting here with you sometimes," she laughed. "You try to get some sleep," she said as she stroked his arm.

"Right," he added. "Miss Winter has some extravagant ideas. That's what's special about her," he smiled. Judith got up and so did Edward.

"Goodnight, Edward," she said. She leaned in and pecked him on the cheek, her soft grey hair brushing the side of his face.

•

Lupin disappeared to check on everyone and then he made his way back downstairs. He roamed through the empty house to Edward's study. He pushed open the door.

"Where are you going?" he asked Edward as Edward did up his duffel coat and put on his hat.

Edward unlocked the cabinet and took out a rifle.

"Out," he said. "I believe there's a werewolf in these parts who's an alpha. If there's blood, it's coming from a human and the wolf is on the prowl. I need to find out what it is, so I can kill it." He pulled back the magazine of the gun.

Lupin shook his head, his thick black hair shining.

"Your guests are suspicious Edward. They think there is a murderer on the loose and who knows; they might just go to the police. That was real blood out there, and we don't know who it belongs to."

"I have to find the alpha male. I can feel its heart pumping. I feel its temptation. I want to get to it first!" Edward brushed Lupin aside and hurried down the long corridor.

Luna watched Edward walking to the front door from the top of the stairs and decided to follow him. She rushed back to her room, trying not to wake Judith who was now fast asleep. She tiptoed around throwing on some clothes and strode out of the room closing the door behind her.

Where are you going, Edward Sampson, at this time of night? she wondered and hurried down the stairs. She popped on her walking boots and shrugged on her coat and hat.

Crunching through the snow Luna, did not know where she was going, but followed the traces of Edward's footprints. It was cold and she rubbed her hands together to keep herself warm. Luna carried on following Edward silently. *Why does he have that gun?*

As she moved further away from the house and into the woodland, the howls unsettled Luna.

CHAPTER 3

INTO THE WOODLAND

The flurries continued to fall and they settled onto the fir trees and onto the ground. Edward paced through the woods trying not to make any sound. A rustling through the bushes kept him on high alert and he turned back and forth, watching just in case someone was coming for him.

The patter of feet came from a fox as it scurried away into the bushes.

"Damn you, fox," he mumbled to himself. He quivered and fought the frozen sensation in his hands which felt like they were turning to ice. He was about to let go of his rifle; his fingers stiff but continued to clench.

Edward plodded along the icy path through the eerie towering trees. He did not make any sound, however the rustling continued coming from amongst the surrounding bushes.

A sudden scream echoed through the forest; a female's voice. Edward moved further into the forest. He kept on moving, twisting, and turning. There he came to a clearing where the figure of a woman lay on the ground. Her clothing, partly covered in snow, looked familiar.

"What on earth are you doing here?" he bellowed.

"I was bored out of my wits in there," Luna replied in pain, reaching for her ankle.

"You must have tripped over that branch." He rolled his eyes. "Can you stand?"

"Yes," she moaned. Edward put down his rifle and helped her up. "What the hell are you doing out here and why have you got that gun?" she asked.

"You shouldn't be out here alone and it's the middle of the night."

"Yes, but I couldn't sleep, so I thought I'd follow you to see what you were up to," she said.

"We're turning back," he replied.

There was a jerk of movement from the direction of the towering overgrown bushes and tangle of brambles.

"What was that?" she said. He pressed his finger to her lips. He snatched up the rifle and held her back.

"We know you're there, so come out," he said.

From behind the bushes, a male figure appeared. He scrambled on his hands and knees, shivering, saliva dripping from his mouth. Luna gasped and hid further behind Edward's shoulder. Edward pointed the rifle at the man.

"Flesh, blood pumping, heart beating," he said, his rough voice making Luna tremble.

She stepped back from Edward. The beast-like creature jumped, pushing Edward to the side and knocking over Luna. He jumped through the icy patches, withdrawing through the forest, faster than a speeding bullet, too fast for Edward to follow.

"What was that?" she yelled.

"Come on, let's get out of here." He strapped the rifle

around his chest and helped the limping Luna back to the house as snow began to fall more heavily.

•

"Lupin, grab some ice for Miss Winter," Edward called as they stumbled into the house.

"What on earth happened?" Lupin asked.

"Tell you in a minute. Hurry, man," Edward cried.

Edward scooped Luna in his arms and carried her to the sofa.

"Oh, thank you," she sighed, breathless from the pain.

"She's had the fright of her life. She's in shock, she's hurt her ankle," Edward said. Lupin placed an ice pack onto her ankle.

"I deserve an explanation," she said, addressing Edward.

"This is ridiculous I am going to call the police-"

"You can't call the police!" Edward shouted. "You saw a werewolf!"

Luna burst into hysterical laughter. "Okay, could you say that again because I didn't think I heard you right."

"You saw an alpha male in the snow this morning looking for its prey. I've been trying to hunt him down," Edward replied.

"You're not joking," she said.

"No, I'm being serious and you have just put yourself and all of us in danger!"

She shook her head. "Oh, don't be silly, Edward, stop

panicking," she exhaled. "Thank you," she said to Lupin, handing back the ice pack. "I think I'll go and freshen up."

"Lupin, help Luna up, will you? Yes, you need to get some rest."

Lupin nodded.

•

Lupin marched down the stairs half an hour later.

"So what did you see?" He sat across from Edward on the sofa.

Edward twiddled his fingers. "I saw him, we saw him. A werewolf… and there must be more. They're here, Lupin, they've arrived."

"So it's true. Come with me… see for yourself, you're the detective in all of this!" Edward followed him into the study where Lupin grabbed a book from the shelf and placed it on Edward's desk.

"Stop!" shouted Edward

"We've got to stop them. We can't let them come in!" Lupin leant back on the mahogany desk, his slender frame in contrast to Edward's bulky form.

"Let's get some rest and follow this up in the morning."

"Yes, you're right let's get some sleep." They both left the room.

Edward took the key from his pocket and locked the study door behind him.

CHAPTER 4
THE JOLLY IN THE WOODS

At breakfast, everyone was quiet until Dr Maloney spoke. He scoffed his marmalade on toast and wiping the crumbs from around his mouth and nestled in his beard, said, "It's interesting what you hear at night. It's kind of mysterious." He slurped his coffee and took another bite.

"Whatever do you mean?" Edward looked up, from his fried breakfast.

"Well, that scuffle outside the front gardens last night? Did you not hear it? Or are you somewhat further back in the house from the rest of us?"

Edward shook his head. "I am as a matter of fact, but we do get foxes and badgers around here," he bemused. "However, Luna tripped and sprained her ankle. She came with me to lock up the main gate," he said, looking at her.

"I wasn't looking where I was going. I'm silly really. Sorry, Edward," she said and continued to munch on her toast.

"Well, I'm looking forward to our jaunt this morning and then tomorrow your presentation Edward," remarked Judith.

"The snow is rather heavy," interrupted Lupin.

"Oh, I think a little snow won't hurt anyone," said Luna. "You and Mr Lupin seem to know the area rather well don't you, and you can lead us."

"Don't worry dear, I was out like a log. Didn't hear a thing, but glad you're okay now. But I agree, I can't wait." Judith clasped her hands together. "We'll get to see the forest at last," she remarked.

Dr Maloney laughed brutishly. "Jaunts and jollies… I'd rather stay in the warm and have more tea, read the morning papers," he said and continued drinking his morning coffee.

"Don't be so pompous," Judith replied, rolling her eyes at him.

"Okay now, be calm, all of you. We'll not go too far in as there's likely to be another heavy snowfall here again later this morning according to the local weather forecast."

As they all left the room, Edward grabbed Luna by the wrist. "What were you thinking suggesting a thing like that?"

"Have you forgotten, Dr Sampson? We suggested this walk last night and you agreed to it before I witnessed that creature in the woods, which, by the way, you've not mentioned to the rest of your guests. And you've not told me exactly what that thing was either or what it was after." She let go of Edward's hand. "Now if you'll excuse me, I need to get ready."

She stormed off like a petulant child.

•

They all gathered in the grand hallway, wearing various degrees of hiking gear and warm clothing that gave the assurance of keeping them warm despite the plunging temperatures.

"Right," called Edward. "The teams are as follows, Justin and Luna with me and Judith and Maloney you're with Lupin. Please keep to the tracks and don't go wandering off." He looked at them like a stern schoolteacher.

They all headed out of the door. "Hmm, the blood seems to have gone," called out Justin.

"Snow keeps falling but there are still signs of blood," replied Luna.

"Let's pick up our pace. The faster we go the quicker we come back," suggested Edward.

"We're not going to get lost now, are we?" Justin called out.

"Scared, Mr Locke?" Luna asked.

"No, just cautious," he replied with chattering teeth.

"Come on." Luna grabbed his arm.

"Don't go tripping up anywhere," he laughed.

"Don't be cheeky," replied Luna. She carried on as Edward and Justin followed her, and everyone parted ways.

•

The car journey seemed to take forever for lovers Patrick Durham and Jill Martin. They stopped along the side of the lonely country lane leading up to the manor's gated entrance. Jill undid her seat belt and leaned into her boyfriend. A sudden jerk outside the car made Jill jump.

"What was that?"

"Could be a fox or something," said Patrick as he moved in for a long slow kiss.

She stopped him. "I heard it again, Patrick," she whispered. "It's coming from the front of the car." She peered through the windscreen. A claw reached up against the glass in front of her. She screamed. She jumped towards her boyfriend. The werewolf smashed the windscreen to smithereens and his beady eyes glared at them both as blood poured from its mouth.

"Get out, get out," screamed Jill.

Patrick tried to open the door but was stopped as another werewolf smashed into his side of the car. The window shattered into a thousand pieces. Shards of glass flew everywhere. The werewolf ripped the car doors off and reached inside the vehicle scratching and biting at their next victims. The screams of Patrick and Jill echoed like thunder across the chilly air.

•

Team one wandered into the forest. "This is so peaceful," said Justin as he looked around.

"I don't know about that," replied Luna.

Edward looked across at her.

"What?"

"Stop right there," Edward snapped.

"Come on, Edward, I'm not a child and neither is Justin, so I think it's about time you just cut the crap and dealt with it," she yelled.

Edward was about to interrupt when there was an unexpected movement ahead of them.

"What was that?" Justin asked.

"Stay here," said Edward.

Deeper into the forest, Edward moved on ahead of them through the snow with his heavily clad feet shuffling against the snow. He brushed away branches and kicked away brambles, cutting his hand in the process.

"Are you okay?" asked Luna as he cussed under his breath.

"It's just a scratch, it will be fine. I, like you said at breakfast, I need to be more careful." He pressed his finger to his lips. He edged closer towards the undergrowth as Luna and Justin stood frozen in fear like statues.

As Edward got nearer, the noise occurred once more. It was just loud enough for Edward to hear. He took out his binoculars from his satchel. His companions ran after him.

"I think we've got it," he bellowed. "Stay close behind me."

"We're going to be too late meeting the others if we don't hurry," she yelled, breaking into a run. "Come on!"

"Don't let me down," he yelled. He then came to the spot. It was too late. He strode towards the car. The victims lay lifeless inside. Luna and Justin gasped as they saw the lifeless young man and woman, their bodies sprawled across the front seats, covered in blood.

•

Piercing screams boomed across the forest.

Dr Maloney bellowed, "What was that!"

Judith screamed.

A man sat on the edge of thick tree branch like Tarzan. Lupin dragged Judith towards him.

"It's a half-naked man, human but not human. He looks different. He's got demon eyes and he's metamorphosing," Dr Maloney boomed.

Lupin looked around for something to defend themselves with.

"It's not a man," he yelled.

"By Jove, what on earth is it then?" Dr Maloney called.

"It's a werewolf," Lupin shouted.

The werewolf jumped down from the tree and roared. Saliva dribbled from his teeth. Sniffing, it stared at them with his beady black eyes.

"What do we do? If we run, it will kill us," shouted Dr Maloney.

"Judith, get behind Maloney," said Lupin.

She hid behind Dr Maloney; the werewolf stared at her.

Dr Maloney quaked like a nervous child.

"Dr Maloney, don't you dare," called Lupin.

"He's going to kill us," Dr Maloney wailed.

"Don't antagonise it," Lupin demanded.

Lupin's face began to boil with anger as the werewolf stared at him before pouncing.

"Lupin!" screamed Judith, her hand covering her wide mouth.

Lupin roared at the beast. Lupin and the werewolf

brawled, grappling in the snow. Judith gasped as Lupin's façade morphed. His body crackled like thunder as his bones shifted. He cried out in pain as his back broadened and his shoulders grew. His posture changed, he slouched and leaned towards the ground. His bones lengthened and popped and stretched through his skin. He continued to wail in agony. Then a thick fur sprung up all over his body. He became unrecognisable. He was turning into something different, nothing she had ever seen before. His mouth was full of gleaming white fangs as his cries pierced the eerie silence. Lupin was… he was a werewolf.

The werewolf struck Lupin with his arm. Lupin threw the werewolf back to the floor, and flung a punch at him. The werewolf shrieked, but he managed to grab Lupin's arm, twisting it back as if making an arrest. Lupin clenched his clawed fists and threw a wild punch into the werewolf's head with ferocious force, knocking the werewolf unconscious.

"Maloney, help me!" Judith screamed, running to Lupin's aid.

The pompous man nodded, hurried over to Lupin and helped him up. Lupin stared confused, unsettled. He looked over to the unconscious creature. "What about that thing there?" Dr Maloney added.

"We've got to leave it. We've got to get Lupin out of here right now before the others in the werewolf pack return. Let's get back to the manor," she said.

CHAPTER 5
RESTLESS

One hour later, a weak Lupin, now human again, sat on the sofa, with Judith. Luna had been pacing up and down the room twiddling her fingers as Justin made notes in his notepad, stopping intermittently to push back his long fringe.

"I think you better put that away, Mr Locke," boomed Dr Maloney, drinking whisky to calm his nerves.

Edward strode through the hall from his office. Luna scorned at him.

"See what's happened," she said, pointing at Lupin.

"You don't know the half of it," said Dr Maloney, shaking his head.

"That is quite enough, Doctor," replied Judith. Justin stood up from the leather sofa and walked over to Edward, his long strides matching his long legs. Edward turned from him, his heart aching with grief as he watched his friend still in pain, in shock.

"You all need to listen to this and you'll need to brace yourselves. Justin, I think you'd better put your pen and paper away because, if you go ahead and publish this you will be arrested," Edward said. "All of you sit down."

Justin put down his pen and paper down onto the coffee table and folded his arms across his broad chest.

"What were those things, Edward?" Luna squealed.

"Luna, I'm sorry not to have told you last night. It's because I didn't know what we were dealing with," Edward said, pacing around the room.

"They were werewolves of a different breed… not only can they roam the night but they are active and hunt during the day." He ran his fingers through his hair. "Lupin turned into one, don't ask me how or why. He must have got bitten at some point in his life and the poison is in him. The toxic must've stayed dormant in him… dormant until now. It's the bacteria in the bite, the werewolf's saliva that activates the transformation… I never knew… poor Lupin," he sighed.

Dr Maloney shot up and stood back from him. "He's a beast… we saw him change into one of those things."

"Yes, but it's more complicated than that. Lupin is but he isn't yet, not really. Lupin is what is referred to as a half-breed werewolf," he replied.

"A half-breed?" asked Judith.

"Yes, half-breed means that he is not a full-grown werewolf. He didn't take in all the bite." Lupin stood up, swaying as if rather giddy.

Dr Maloney stood up and stood back towards the bookshelves.

"Dr Maloney, please sit down. I am not now, nor will I ever be, a werewolf," cried Lupin.

"Yes, but I saw you, you changed right in front of us," shouted back Dr Maloney.

"Sit down, you fool!" Luna shouted at Dr Maloney.

"Don't you dare talk to me like that, you silly girl. I

am not staying here!" Dr Maloney rushed out into the hallway, towards the staircase. "If you go out there then they will kill you, Maloney," bellowed Justin after him.

"Well, you are all fools then for staying here and what do you think you are going to do by staying here, ha? I'm leaving and going to call for the police, and they will come here and arrest you all," Dr Maloney's voice echoed. Edward's temples felt like they were going to explode. He followed Dr Maloney up the spiral staircase to his room.

"You've got to calm down so that we can talk!" Edward called out, following him into the bedroom.

"This is a damn debacle of a weekend, Sir!" Dr Maloney shouted back.

Dr Maloney found his luggage carrier and threw it on to the bed. Opening it, he grabbed everything he could get easily and stuffed his case. He stopped, turned round to the windowpane; two glaring eyes stared back at him through the darkness.

Dr Maloney's bellowing scream pierced the whole household. He scrambled to the door and made his way down the corridor and down the stairs.

Edward, only after hesitating for a split second, hurried after him.

Dr Maloney kept looking back as the eyes followed him, and he stumbled and fell all the way down the staircase, hitting his head on the floor.

Edward rushed over to him and knelt down. He checked for a pulse. He looked at the others. "Maloney!" he shouted.

•

Edward carried Maloney with the help of Justin, Luna and Judith down to the wine cellar. He gestured to the table in the middle of the room. Cases and barrels full of wines from around the world were stacked along the floor and up to the top of the low ceiling filling the cellar with the strong smell of grapes. They placed Maloney's body on the table, and placed a table cloth over it.

"Stupid, pompous fool," Edward mumbled to himself. He looked at the others.

"He should've listened to me. This thing is in the grounds. I'm sure of it," he said to them. "We need to make sure the place is barricaded so that the beasts, these werewolves won't get in. No one is allowed to leave this place, do you understand me?"

The men and women nodded. Edward gestured to his friends to leave the cellar.

One by one they headed up the staircase back to the main part of the manor.

•

In the cold silence of the cellar, Dr Maloney's eyes opened. He threw the cloth to the floor and stared at the ceiling. The barred windowpane broke and smashed to smithereens. Two werewolves pulled away the iron security bars and bundled into the wine cellar. They began to paw over the body, sniffing Maloney from head to foot. One of the creatures bit into him as he lay there. They stared as within minutes Maloney's body began to morph into a beast.

"Come with us, feed with us," they said as one.

The wolf creatures moved in a pack and stuck close together. In the distance, they heard the human voices. They scrambled through the windowpane and scurried faster into the forest beyond the manor.

•

As dusk settled, Judith retired to her bedroom. She passed Edward in the corridor. "Ah there you are," she said, holding a glass full of whisky.

"Are you okay?" he asked.

"Yes, I'm just going to make a few calls," she replied. "Take my mind off all this banality."

Edward looked down at her drink.

"To calm my nerves," she said.

"I'm glad you're here and accepted the invitation," he reassured, holding her hand.

"Edward I always admired your spirit and charm and your knowledge about everything… you know and understand so much more than any of us about things going bump in the night. You'll find answers you're looking for," she said.

"Do you think?" he asked quite surprised.

"I don't know how you came to acquire the manor

and how Lupin fits into all this but I don't care. You're unique," she said.

"I will take that as a compliment." His cheeks flushed with embarrassment.

"Good, I'm glad. Well, if you would excuse me for now, I'll be back down shortly." She moved towards him, pecked him on the cheek, and paced along the corridor to her room. Edward touched his cheek, blushing a little, before turning to join the others downstairs.

CHAPTER 6
MISSING

That evening after dinner, Edward was in his study. Lupin walked into the room, now fully recovered after resting, and saw the photo of Dr Maloney pinned on the wall.

"If only he had listened," said Edward.

"It's not your fault man," replied Lupin as he stood back and looked at Edward.

"He's yet another victim. We have to somehow stop them," Edward said as he buried his head in his hands.

"We are going to do that together," Lupin said as he touched Edward's shoulder.

Edward looked back at Lupin as he sat back against his chair. "We'll do this together and with the help of the others. Get the others in here. They need to know about my work in the black arts and my involvement in demonology studies. It's time to be honest. To share all I know. It's only fair."

•

Justin, Luna and Judith followed Lupin into the study minutes later.

"This is where you write your books then, Mr Sampson," Justin said.

Luna stared at his working wall, pictures of people on

his board amongst werewolves, demonic beings and other ghouls.

"Why do you have these photos of people?" Judith asked, folding her arms. She looked around her and looked more closely at his working wall.

"I am a demonologist. I study the unexplained," he said, picking up a book from his desk.

"What you see are missing people. I've also added Dr Maloney's picture since his death and this is *The Howling*," he said. He opened the book-marked and read it aloud to everyone. "Let the Alpha bite his prey and the Alpha bite extradite the human in its pack. The fear in you is what they seek and the boiling blood is what they drink. They feed forever a pack beyond our reach." He shut the book with a thump which startled Luna.

"So how do we destroy a werewolf?" Justin asked, scratching his stubble.

"I heard shooting it with silver bullets is one way but there are many other ways too such as with mercury or with incantations." said Judith.

"These werewolves are half breed that can be seen in daylight as well." Edward raised his eyes at them.

"Now look at the wall."

"What are we supposed to be looking for?" interrupted Judith

"We have to be clear. I want you to look at bite marks, how the human changes after an attack? After metamorphosing and the after effects," Edward said.

"What about you, Lupin? You were changing into one

of them. What triggers man to morph into a werewolf?" she asked.

"You seem to know about these, creatures Luna," said Judith.

"I was up for a movie once, Into The Werewolf's Eyes," she replied.

"Well, this is not a movie now," Edward snapped. "This is reality."

"I know." She rolled her eyes back at him.

"It's like an electric shock initially. Your whole body changes form and it hurts like hell. It's awful. It's the worst pain you can imagine but have no control over what is happening. You're suddenly, within minutes, not yourself anymore… you're a demon and it's horrible!" Lupin said trembling.

Lupin turned to the board of victims. "Look at them. Some are dead… they're the lucky ones. They can't morph once they're dead. It will not surprise me if there are more out there. We need to know if the bodies are missing, which means they are out there and could be increasing the werewolf pack or still in the morgue."

Edward picked up the phone and dialled.

"Can I speak to Dr Joanne Howard please?" he said. "It's Edward Sampson." He waited, drumming his fingers on the desk with impatience while the others just stared. "Joanne, it's your favourite friend," he beamed, his narrow eyes twinkling. "Joanne, I know you've helped me in the past with things out of the ordinary and I need your help again." He pressed his finger on the loudspeaker button so everyone could hear the rest of the conversation. "The bodies that were brought to you the other day," he said.

"What about them?" she asked.

"Have you still got them?" Edward winced.

"Yes we have. They've not been signed out or collected by the undertakers," she said with an unnerving tone. "Why?"

"I need you to check them for me, to see if they are still actually there in the morgue."

"Not going to ask why but okay. I will give you a ring back," she said, hanging up.

They all found a space in the study and sat or stood, with reference books in their laps or in their hands. The phone rang within minutes. Edward jumped from his seat and picked up the phone.

"Hello," he answered. "Joanne… tell me the worst."

"The bodies, they're gone!"

Edward paused.

"Edward, Edward, are you there?" she gasped. "Tell me what I need to do; I have bodies missing from the morgue!"

"Don't panic. Let me think. I'll contact the officials about this okay? Don't do anything," he reassured, putting down the receiver.

"Now what?" asked Justin.

Edward got up from his desk, brushed past the others and out the door. Judith marched after him.

"Edward, Edward, what's the matter?" Judith called out after Edward who ran like a wild cheetah down the corridor to the cellar.

Edward gasped. He slammed his fists onto the table.

"Edward. Where's Dr Maloney? Where's his body?" Judith gasped.

Edward spun round and shouted. "The body's gone. They've taken him. The werewolves. There's no other explanation." He looked ahead to the cellar's smashed window, the evidence clear.

•

It was after 8:30pm, and everyone seemed exhausted as they gathered in the lounge, Lupin handed everyone cups of strong black coffee. The strong odour made Justin's hazel eyes open a little wider.

Luna inhaled the whiff, and slurped as fast as she could, after pouring a dash of cream into her cup and stirring. She was eager for a cigarette.

"Okay," Lupin said. "I know what I need to do." He handed the last two cups to Judith and Edward. "I have to somehow call the pack together. Be one of them," he said.

Judith drank a little of her coffee and placed the cup down onto the coffee table. "No, it'll put you in danger," she gasped. "I can be the bait... get them to come to us."

"No," said Edward. "No one will be bait and put their lives in danger. We've lost Maloney and I don't want to lose any of you."

"We can't just sit here and do nothing when there are creatures out there hunting and killing innocent people," snapped Justin.

"Look everyone, we are all tired, it's late, we need some sleep. It looks like Edward could have a plan here to stop these creatures, but we have to trust him now. He knows what he's doing," said Luna somewhat hastily.

"Luna's right, let's get some rest," Justin said.

They all headed to their rooms apart from Lupin and Edward.

"That girl does make some sort of sense you know," Lupin said. "She's not as bad as they say she is." He patted Edward on his shoulder. "Get some rest," he said.

•

Tossing and turning in his sleep, Lupin thrashed about as if fighting werewolf apparitions of the pack; images of the werewolves danced around him, blood dripped from their mouths and dried in congealed clumps on the thick tufty fur of their muscular bodies. They seemed to be drowning in blood; a vicious waterfall of red.

His body began to sweat and his eyes opened wide. They bulged and burned like roaring fire. The howls became louder and louder booming in his head and then filled the room as they escaped his own mouth, now wide and full of sharp fangs.

Lupin's body began to morph; he changed from man to wolf and the pain of the transformation tore through him like a storm.

CHAPTER 7
AWAKENING

Lupin's body was no longer his; a demon had woken up inside of him. It possessed him. He crawled over to the window, his shoulders hunched over, and watched the snowfall. He threw his fist at the window, smashing it with one huge almighty crash; he leapt out and landed on all fours on the soft inches of snow.

The pack stood poised and ready to jump in at him. They sniffed, moving in closer to him and pawed around him. They hissed at him. The pack was ready for the kill. Lupin too was now no more than a wild animal and he was ready for his prey.

The wolf men scarpered off into the distance, howling through the flurries. Looking down on them, a robed Edward gazed through his bedroom window as they hurried off into the stretch of open land ahead. He had a strange feeling and held his stomach as butterflies churned inside of him. He rushed out of his bedroom in the eves and ran as fast as he could down the flight of stairs to the bedrooms where he knocked on Lupin's bedroom door.

"Lupin, are you there?" he bellowed. Judith opened her bedroom door and peered round in her checked pyjamas.

"What is this racket, Edward?" she said, stifling a yawn. Edward looked back. "Don't worry, go back to bed."
She rolled her eyes. "I can't sleep now," she replied.

Edward continued to knock on Lupin's door but there was no answer. He then used his elbow and shoved with all his might; the door swung open.

Edward barged in to find the window smashed and Lupin's bed empty.

Judith walked in behind him and gasped at the empty bed and the tangle of bed linen.

"They've taken him. The wolves have got into Lupin's mind," he shouted. "I told him not to turn but he did. He couldn't fight it. What is he playing at? Damn it." He hurried out of the door and Judith ran after him.

•

Judith, unable to sleep, had got dressed and made breakfast for everyone in Lupin's absence.

"Nice eggs," remarked Luna as she chomped on them.

"Thank you, I do like cooking," Judith said drinking her coffee.

"Two people are now missing and no one's doing anything about it," remarked Justin.

"I understand your frustration Justin but I have to go through certain channels to proceed with the matter," Edward said. "Now please excuse me." He stood up abruptly and left the room.

Luna leaned over. "Well done, Justin," she glared.

Edward marched along to his study, locked himself in and stared at the wall displaying all the victims. He then studied the books on his shelf. He picked out *'The Howling'* and sitting at his desk, flipped through the pages. He found another paragraph he had previously studied and ran his fingers over the lines reading to himself. "Let the Alpha bite his prey and let the Alpha extradite the human from the pack, hmm," he muttered. He rubbed his forehead. He felt rather sleepy, as he had not slept at all well the previous night. He yawned a little and placed his head down onto the table. Sleep took over and he drifted off to sleep.

•

Hikers were walking in the snow the next day. Snow fell to the ground. They laughed and chatted as they navigated their way through the forest.

"Hey mate, this is an awesome find," said one of them as they looked ahead.

"You can see mountains galore from here," said another as they moved on.

"I think we'd all better stick to the path." They all nodded and agreed. They heard a crackling of broken twigs from the bushes around them and tiptoed ahead.

"What was that?" said a female who was wearing a multi-coloured bobble hat.

"Oh, most probably an animal," said the man carrying a rucksack. "You find all sorts round here," he said. They moved forward, a high pitched wail filtered through the area.

"That's not an animal," she shrieked as the others laughed on ahead.

"Do you want to hold my hand?" said the man.

She nodded, grabbing it.

"I can see you," a voice said.

"Cut it out," she snapped.

"I didn't say anything. It could be James being stupid. You know what he's like," he said to her. Another cry bellowed through the woods.

"James! James, is that you?" the young man yelled.

They rushed ahead, and they spotted James.

"James!" shrieked the girl.

He climbed the tree from branch to branch and sat firmly on one of its wide boughs. "What a view from up here," he said as he looked around taking in the scenery. "The vast countryside is beautiful with all its little houses spread out."

"We'll get you down," she said. "Stop messing around."

Before she could do anything, the body of their friend was swiped right before their eyes from the branch he sat on and whatever had taken him quickly disappeared, deeper into the thick canopy of the trees above.

The girl screamed. A body dropped to the floor in front of her. She screamed again. She gasped and fled followed by the other lad. Running faster and faster like the wind.

"James!" she continued shouting. She gasped and screamed louder than ever.

"Wolves," the other young man yelled.

They ran faster but the sound of the howls closed in on them.

The young female heard screams around her. It was too late as a pack jumped in front of her and howled around her. Six werewolves licked their lips as blood dripped like saliva from their fanged jaws. They were ready to feast.

The young man slipped to the floor as the werewolves danced around sniffing, at him, hissing and gnashing, one of them wiping blood from its teeth.

He grabbed at the rock next to him to pull himself up and scrambled away from the werewolves' lair. His boots sank into the snow as he tried to get away, to get somewhere, anywhere but here. But they kept coming after him, he could hear the howl calling out to him.

A werewolf's hand hurtled him towards the tree opposite the cave. Like an avalanche, the snow from above fell down on top of him like a ton of bricks. He brushed the flurries away from him like dust. He got up again, and pounced onto the creature; with all his might he kneed it in the stomach.

"Get away from her!" the young man screamed.

The werewolf lunged its hand towards him once again and with one flick of its claw slit the throat of the man. He fell to the ground, his eyes open wide, listless, and dead with fright. The girl escaped, and she crawled away like a baby, her fingers digging deep into the snow but another hand reached out, then another and then another and her screams filled the forest with a forbidden haunting.

CHAPTER 8
THE CALLING

Judith opened the door to Edward's office. "Knock, knock. It's me," she said, peering round the door.

"Hey, Judith." Edward looked up from his desk.

"You've not gone to bed at all. I just made some vegetable soup as Lupin's still not here," she sighed, putting the tray down on Edward's desk.

"Thank you, but I don't need anything."

"Have you found anything that could help us fight these werewolves?" she asked, twiddling her fingers as she paced around the room.

"The usual silver bullets…" Edward pushed the piles of papers to one side of his desk. "Silver bullets or blades," he said. "We'll get them with those. We'll entice them with our scent and our fresh blood and they will come to us. We will kill them ourselves."

"So how do we do that exactly?" she asked.

The mobile on Edward's desk began to ring.

"Hello? Joanne?" he said. "Joanne, yes, I'm here… what's the matter? Thank you for letting me know… we'll be there as soon as possible." Edward stood putting his mobile in his back pocket.

"What's wrong?" asked Judith.

"There have been more murders in the forest… not far

from the manor's boundary. Joanne's there now," he said as he headed towards the door.

"Where are you going?" she asked.

"Going to see Joanne. It's important," he called out.

"Justin, Luna and I are coming with you," demanded Judith.

"Those creatures are out there and if they want to find you, they will have to come to us first."

"Don't follow me!" he snapped.

Justin and Luna stood in the doorway listening in and they both stepped aside as Edward brushed past them.

"Where's he going?" Luna asked.

"Somewhere where he shouldn't go alone. Come on!" Judith cried. "But blundering and going all guns blazing won't solve anything. Let me go and talk to him," she added. "Stay here and I will come back once he changes his mind."

Judith chased Edward and finally caught up with him. "Don't go anywhere just yet," she said, puffed out from chasing him.

"Are you going to give me the third degree now?"

"You can do what you want but you need your friends. You need us to keep you sane or you will do something you regret," she remarked. "Now you wait here and I'll go and get the others. You're not going anywhere without us," she said, dangling the car keys in front of him as he slipped on his duffel coat.

•

The 4x4 drove up the lane to the outer boundary of the forest. Edward had his windscreen wipers on; the snow was coming down heavier.

"Look there," said Justin as they approached the murder scene.

Edward cut the engine.

"Joanne?" He almost didn't recognise her; her usually long flowing hair was tucked under a plastic cap and her mouth concealed by a face mask.

Joanne Dean peered from the crime scene in a forensic suit. Two uniformed officers stood in front of the area taped off with crime scene tape; one seemed to be keeping a log of the people coming and going. Crime scene photographers efficiently and silently took photographic evidence of the corpses, careful where they were stepping so as not to contaminate anything that may give them a clue as to what had happened. Forensic science technicians were gathering evidence from the bodies and from the surrounding area.

Joanne walked over towards him and took her mask off. "Edward," she said and shook his hand.

"Joanne Dean, I'd like you to meet my guests Judith Hale, Justin Locke and Luna Winter."

She smiled at all of them. "I can't show you what I've found here but what I'm about to tell you is not for the faint-hearted."

"Only Edward is allowed to come in," she nodded and led Edward through the crime scene barrier while the others moved away and waited.

A stench hung in the air; the stench of death and panic and horror. Judith shivered.

"Right. Time of death, I assume, around midday. There are deep bite marks around the neck, some scratches, likely from an animal... claws. The eyes are scratched all over and perpetrated. Young man... in his twenties. Over here... a female, similar sort of age. Ripped from the insides and again the same type of scratches around the eyes... look at them."

Edward looked closely and examined the bodies of the young male and female shred to bits. Edward's stomach churned. "I feel as though whatever I've eaten is about to come out." He coughed, almost retched and took a deep breath looking back again. He paced around the bodies. "Take a look at this here," he coughed again. "Look at that... a splinter of something... from a sharp claw? Did you notice that?" He pointed.

"Let me see," she said.

"Around the neck, Joanne, look closely."

Joanne knelt down. She gestured for the forensic photographers to come over. "Take this and look for anymore deep cuts round the neck."

The man and woman nodded.

•

Edward was in his office studying the paper work on his desk. He looked at his clock; it was 3pm. There was a knock at the door.

"Come in," he said.

Justin entered with a tray. "Hello, I thought you might be in need of some nourishment." He laid it down on a side table next to his desk. "Soup, eat up before it gets cold." He smiled and asked, "What are you looking at?"

"Incantations, spells, dark magic. Things to entice the werewolves or bring all this terror to an end," said Edward.

"We have to find a way to avoid harm coming to anyone else. We need to bring these monsters to us."

"We already-"

"I don't want another death," interrupted Edward, twiddling his fingers in agitation.

There was a sudden scream.

"The girls," boomed Justin and they both fled out of the office.

•

In the sitting room, the girls sat back against the back of the couch, as if wanting to be absorbed by its fabric.

"What happened? What's wrong?" said Justin, taking in the terror in their eyes. Luna pointed to the window a trembling finger.

Edward paced up to the window and examined the red blood sprawled all over the glass that said 'KILL'. Edward lightly touched the windowpane, the glass shattered to pieces, destroying the evidence they had. A gust of wind blew out the lit candles on the coffee table.

•

Justin helped Edward board up the window later that evening. "There that should hold it," said Edward tapping the board.

"Was that a warning?" Justin gulped.

"Maybe," suggested Edward.

There was a cough from behind. "I think Luna was more terrified than I was," replied Judith as she was tying her robe tighter around her waist.

"Why did they not come in?" agonised Edward.

"You didn't invite them in, that's the thing. Like vampires, right? You need to let them inside. You told us these werewolves are of a different breed all together," said Judith. She looked at the boarded window.

"Is that safe?"

"Boarded and nailed down," Justin said.

"That time you were surrounded with Luna, did anyone scratch you?" Justin umm'ed and ahh'ed.

"Not that I know of," he said. He rolled up his sleeves and looked at his arms.

"Do you think you could go and get Luna for me please, Judith," said Edward.

•

Judith hurried to the room she was now sharing with Luna.

"Luna, Luna, it's Judith," she said.

Luna's bed had not been slept in but the sound of rushing water filled the room. She pushed open the bathroom door and pulled back the curtain around the bath.

"Luna, why didn't you respond when I called you?" said Judith, closing her eyes and turning away from her bathing friend.

Luna covered herself with the shower curtain. "What are you doing here?"

Judith retreated from the bathroom. "Don't worry, don't worry. We need you downstairs, that's all," reassured Judith.

"Okay, okay, give me a second, bloody hell," she called.

CHAPTER 9
ANOTHER SHOCK

Justin bought in coffee and tea. He was finding his way around the place in Lupin's absence. Seeing the fright on Luna's face and the bloodstained window, he burst out, "What a nightmare."

This was really happening. Werewolves had targeted him and his friends. He could, he supposed, use this as an anchor for a great story. However, would anyone believe him?

"Here we go," he said, placing the tray down onto the coffee table.

"A cigarette, anyone?" asked Luna as she pulled a packet from her pocket.

Edward looked up from his laptop and shook his head.

"What are you doing?" asked Judith as she poured out a coffee and added cream.

The doorbell rang interrupting Edward. "Just stay here, please."

"Who is it?" he called, walking towards the front door.

"It's Joanne."

Edward unbolted the door and hugged Joanne.

"Did anyone see you as you drove up here?"

She shook her head as he closed the door behind her. "No one," she yelped.

"Did you bring everything?"

"Yes what I could find in a hurry but I have a feeling that my place would be ram-sacked too," she said. "We will begin as soon as possible. We have the promised lunar light of another full moon. This is likely to impact their behaviour. This is when we can entice the pack to come together," she gasped.

•

Edward led Joanne to the sitting room. "Everyone, you remember Joanne?" They smiled apprehensively and nodded their welcome.

"Hello again. Would you like a coffee or tea?" asked Judith, feeling as though she had turned from doctor to housekeeper.

"Er, no thank you," Joanne smiled, flicking her long hair over her shoulder.

Judith poured another for herself.

"Everyone, I've got more to say to you," Edward said.

"Oh no, not more surprises," Luna rolled her dark eyes.

"I think we've seen a lot of horror the past day or two," Edward sighed.

"Nothing surprises me anymore," Justin glared.

"Very well," he said, "I brought Joanne in as she is not only a forensic pathologist but a master in the arts," he said.

"Oh wow, an artist," exclaimed Luna. "I love Michelangelo."

"Not that kind of arts, Luna, dark arts. Witchcraft… magic."

Luna picked up her cup of coffee and downed what was left, leaving a red lipstick mark around its rim.

"My aim is to bring one of the werewolves back here to us and see if I can extradite the demon within them," said Joanne.

"Yes, but Maloney is as dead as a dodo," gawped Justin.

"No, but not Lupin, he is still as much human as he is beast… if we lure them into the light of the moon then we can revert the process."

"Then let's do it," suggested Judith.

"Where do we begin?" asked Edward.

"Using the tracking devices I have, we will be able to detect where they are hiding. Grab as many cross bows and silver weapons as possible so that we can kill any in our path," Joanne said. Edward nodded.

CHAPTER 10
THE INCANTATION

Like cotton wool, the snow settled down on the ground creating a serene and peaceful setting. Wrapped up warm, Edward took out various gadgets from the bag in the back of the 4x4's boot.

"We've got to do this the right way," said Edward as he began switching on the detector tools. Joanne looked around with her infrared camera. Judith, Luna and Justin were setting up the thermography cameras and torches. Edward taught Judith, Luna and Justin how to switch everything on.

Justin looked at the piece of equipment he had. "Looks more like a jigsaw puzzle. How will all of this get them here?" Justin asked.

"I told you Joanne will entice them to us using the incantation and will bring forth the entire clan," Edward said.

He turned to Joanne who was building a fire. She quickly added tinder and kindling to the centre. She then threw in a handful of cloves and cumin.

She muttered to herself and the fire began to flicker. Her hair shone golden brown in the growing light of the flames.

"What's she saying?" asked Luna, whispering to Edward's ear.

"She's chanting… making way for the gateway to open. So that she can communicate with the werewolves," he whispered.

"Communicating with werewolves?" Luna said.

"Some say they are from another dimension," he replied.

"Well, we're all set," said Judith. She watched Joanne hovering close to the fire with her eyes closed, chanting away. She swayed back and forth on her heels. "It's like she's being taken over. Should we be worried?"

"We must not antagonise her or the incantation won't work," Edward said. "There are rules regarding how many times we can do this." His eyes were fixated on Joanne.

Joanne then opened her eyes and walked around the fire first clockwise and then anti-clockwise… once, twice, three times. Her chanting became louder and louder. Her eyes pierced red reflecting the flames of the fire now roaring and rising higher and higher. She suddenly stopped, rose, and hovered over the fire; smoke rose into the moonlit sky towards the moon.

Luna buried her head in Justin's chest as he shielded her from the heat of the gleaming flames.

"She's speaking another language," Justin whispered. The fire rose higher into the sky.

Joanne howled as she stepped into the fire, and she howled once more as the flames lapped around her and consumed her. Her hair seemed to be on fire. Then the fire dispersed around her. She fell to the ground; unconscious but with no scars and no burns.

"Quick, get her," Edward called. Justin ran over with Edward and knelt to the ground towards a limp Joanne. "Joanne, Joanne, can you hear me?" Edward felt for a pulse.

"Well?" asked Justin.

"She's still alive, but barely responding. We have to take her back to the manor with us."

Luna and Judith stood, gasping with fear.

"This won't work," said Judith.

"Judith, Judith, where are you going?" shouted Edward.

"My God, she's going to get herself killed," roared Luna, her face full of panic, her cheeks streaming with floods of tears.

She gasped, as Joanne changed form.

"What, what?" Edward pulled Justin back as if he was tugging on a rope and flung himself towards Luna.

"What the devil…?" Justin shouted.

"I am invincible," Joanne bellowed. She stretched and breathed in the smoke of the dying embers.

"What have you done with Joanne?" cried Edward.

"She is here, she has woken me. I knew she would come in the end. Someone had to give her a little push." The being that had taken over Joanne stood up and pushed Edward to the side.

"I taunted her, taunted her in her sleep and spoke to her," the voice said as it droned on deeper and deeper. Joanne's body rose from the ground. She began getting taller and taller, her face began to shift and her body formed into something new, something quite monstrous yet remarkably beautiful and mighty.

"Oh no. I should have realised it all along," Edward burst out. "Joanne is the Alpha! Judith has just got herself killed."

•

Judith clenched her fists, running through the vast forest, her feet stamping and crunching in the snow. She paused for a moment catching her breath; she knew she had to get the werewolves' attention so that she could send them out to be trapped by the others.

The werewolves' yowls grew louder and louder. One werewolf jumped from the treetops. Judith was face to face with him. The beast snarled at her. She shook her head and kicked snow towards its face, and then ran. The werewolf roared, hissed, and using its super human strength, it chased her, its next victim, through the forest.

Judith hid behind a great bush. She sat curled up in a ball and tried not to move. The creature scoured the area and sniffed the air. It darted from bush to bush however; it could not see or even smell his victim; Judith's strong perfume was too overpowering.

Judith thought for a moment and then had an idea. She snapped a branch from the tree like a wild animal, rolled up her sleeve, and sliced her hand; blood oozed out.

She ran out waving her arm, drops of blood scattering everywhere. She heard the werewolves' howls in the distance. They seemed to be getting closer and closer and Judith knew she now had them in her grasp.

A werewolf as tall as anything she had ever seen jumped in front of her. Its beady eyes stared right back at her; it reached out to her. She placed her bleeding arm out in front of the wolf creature, taunting it.

"Go on, you want me, don't you? You know you can't resist," she snapped. She reached for a log in the snow and grasped it in her other hand. "Go on then, you want me? Come and get me."

The beast leapt onto her and the log fell out of her hand; she fell to the ground in a defenceless heap. The werewolf towered over her, its breaths coming fast but it just looked at her and turned. It slithered away. She looked up, panting for breath, full of relief.

"Lupin, is that you?" She got up onto her knees and looked more closely at the creature. "Lupin, if it's you, you need to give me a nod," she said. "Lupin, it's you," she gasped. "Does this change hurt you?"

He nodded.

"Let's get you out of here," she said.

CHAPTER 11
THE UNWANTED GUESTS

Edward drove the 4x4 back to the mansion as an unconscious Joanne lay in the back alongside an alert Luna. As he switched off the ignition, he got out, opened the back door and carried Joanne to the house. Justin unlocked the door ahead of them and stood aside to let them in.

"The thing inside of her is going to wake up any moment," shouted Justin.

"She's moving, look," said Luna as she shut and bolted the door.

"We will tie her up," Edward snapped back. They headed to the kitchen, and propped her up on a wooden chair. "There should be some rope or something in the drawer or somewhere there," Edward said, as Joanne began to stir in front of him.

Justin rummaged through the drawers. He found some rope, and tied her arms and legs to the chair. They stood back.

"She won't get out of that," said Edward. He paced up and down. "How could I not have seen this?"

"You weren't to expect it. We didn't and now, now everything is going crazy and it's soon going to be dawn," called Luna.

"What's that tapping?" Justin said.

"Grab anything sharp you can from the drawers!" said Edward. "No prisoners."

Justin grabbed two kitchen knives. He handed one to Luna, and they gripped one in each of their hands.

"Edward walked towards the back door.

"Judith!" Edward was relieved as well as shocked, Judith stood freezing in the doorway covered in mud, blood, and grit.

"Where did you go? You had us worried and look at you. Are you hurt?" Edward said, pulling her indoors.

"It's all right, I'm all right," she slurred, before collapsing on the kitchen floor.

"What's wrong?" he said.

Beady eyes glared through the widow. Luna belted a scream and dropped the knife to the floor. The window smashed as a wolf-man landed in the kitchen, sending the kitchen table flying across the floor with a kick of its leg.

Justin grabbed the wolf from behind. However, Justin was thrown to the floor and he hit his head against the cupboard door.

"No!" screamed Judith. "Don't antagonise him. Look at him."

"You know who it is," she said.

"I know who it is," Edward's eyes were transfixed onto the werewolf.

"Lupin?"

Lupin nodded as he looked to the floor where Justin lay in a daze. Luna held a wet damp towel to the side of Justin's head.

"Lupin, it is you." Edward gazed at his dear friend, now a monster. There was some good in him still, there just had to be. He went over to him and touched Lupin's furry skin, damp with sweat and the chill of the snow. The tall creature knelt towards him on all fours, like a pet to his master.

A shudder came from the chair. Judith screamed as she saw Joanne rise getting taller and taller. Lupin grabbed Judith by the throat. Laughter boomed from Joanne as she morphed into a werewolf; her cries of pain and agony filled the kitchen and rang through the empty manor and beyond.

"Power, invincible. I have the power of a witch and werewolf combined. No one can defeat me," she bellowed.

"Lupin, put her down, you're killing her." Edward grabbed a chair and lunged it at Lupin.

Lupin crushed the chair with his powerful clawed hand, grabbed Edward by the arm, and threw him against the fridge.

Lupin let go of Judith and she fell to the floor.

"Do not toy with me," boomed Joanne.

The whole house shook like an earthquake.

"Power of the moon, power of the earth, power below and above. Come to me my children. Come to me!"

Edward rubbed his forehead and looked at his hand. Blood oozed out. He crawled towards the cupboard to push himself up from the floor.

"Stop right there," he shouted.

"You're feeble. You can't touch me… none of you can. I am invincible and only I can feel the power."

Joanne pushed him back once more, and Edward fell to the floor.

Justin turned to Luna. "Edward told me there are weapons hidden under the desk in the study," he whispered in her ear. She looked at the creature taunting Edward and nodded to Justin. She crawled towards the half-open door and when she was safely on the other side of the door she got up on her hands and knees, stood upright and ran straight for the study where she locked herself inside.

•

"Nice one, under the floorboards. Cliché, like in the movies." She rolled her eyes. She stamped her feet onto the floorboards to find the hollow space. She found a spot. She swiped the red patterned rug aside and fell to her knees. She grabbed hold of the floorboard with both hands and pulled it up, breaking a nail in the process.

She lifted up a wooden chest that reminded her of the kind that would house pirate's treasure. She opened it and found a number of daggers, swords and other weapons. She remembered how the werewolves could be defeated by a silver sword to extradite the demon. "Let's hope this is the right one," she pleaded, grabbing the biggest sabre.

She dragged it out of the wooden box and as she did so, the window smashed behind her.

"Ahh no!" she bellowed. The beady eyes glared at her and the howl of the werewolf made her skin crawl. She lifted the heavy sword and plunged it at him with all her might, knocking him over. "Sorry if it's you, Lupin!" She ran out of the study.

The werewolf ran after her panting and snarling. He smashed everything to pieces as he went along the corridor. Luna did not look back, but kept on running towards the kitchen area. The werewolf flung himself at Luna and pushed her to the ground just as she reached the door to the kitchen.

Joanne turned to Luna. "You little tramp!" she shouted.

"Who are you calling a tramp? You freak!" Luna yelled back, like an argument between two teenage girls in the playground. Joanne swiped her ankle, and Luna fell to the floor as the sword flew towards Edward. "Is that all you can do witch wolf?"

Luna got up, grabbed a kitchen chair and threw it at her.

Edward grabbed the sword from the floor and hurled himself at the werewolf chanting,

"I call thee demons from the underworld
I call thy spirits to unfold
I sacrifice the alpha and extradite to your world."

Joanne's face boiled like thunder.

"I sacrifice this demon to you and avenge thy foe."

Edward stabbed Joanne in her stomach. "I'm sorry," he yelled.

CHAPTER 12
JUDITH'S BEDSIDE

Around midday, Judith sat up in bed with a cup of tea in her hand. Edward, Justin, and Luna sat around her.

"So that is that," said Edward.

"So it would seem." She looked glumly at Edward. "Aren't you smart? You won't be practicing the dark arts anytime soon again now, will you?" she said.

"Now, I think I'll leave that to the experts," Edward replied.

"Well, I won't be forgetting all of this in a hurry," said Luna.

"I thought I was going to come for a jolly weekend with drinks, fun and games and I ended up being chased," Judith said, stroking Edward's hand as it rested on the duvet.

"We need to leave Judith to sleep, I think," said Edward.

"You're right and I need to think of where I can get away to… somewhere quiet after all this pandemonium," Luna said, shaking her head, her usually lustrous hair matt and lifeless.

"On holiday?" piped Justin. "I'll come with you, you know for moral support," he nodded.

She looked at the others and looked back at Justin whose face was like a loved up teenage boy. "Oh, go on then. I'd love you to join me." Luna got up from her seat, and she grabbed Justin's arm. "First class flight, I think. My treat and we deserve it. I think we saved the world."

"That was the film *Into The Unknown* right?" Justin said as they left Judith to rest.

"Oh yeah," she replied cheekily.

"Well, I think love could be in the air," Judith managed a weak smile. "You brought everyone together, you know that?"

"You think. We lost two people. How can that bring us together?" Edward, sighed.

"Because you held it together to the end. Think of that pompous brute, Maloney. He was a fool but you had Lupin and Joanne's back. You revealed their good side," she yawned.

"You're tired. You need rest," Edward said, stroking her face.

"Once you are up and about Doctor Hale, can I ask you to dinner?"

CHAPTER 13
THE BOOK LAUNCH

A few days later, Edward stood in the conference room in Justin's newspaper headquarters. Even though he originally planned to unveil his new book in front of his friends at home, had suggested the book be promoted in a different way. The room was filled with photographers and TV camera operators much to Edward's delight. Justin had generously organised a press conference to announce the release of Edward's new book.

As people began to arrive, they chatted and admired copies of Edward's book on display at various points around the room.

Edward stood twiddling his fingers as he looked at the number of people present for his book launch. Although he had experienced this kind of crowd at university and on his tours at the museum, he did not expect such a turnout. He blamed Justin, but knew too that he had done this as a thank you for saving his life as well as the lives of the others.

Luna looked dazzling in a beaded 1920s evening gown; her hair shone and her eyes sparkled as she handed out glasses of champagne and nibbles with Judith. Judith wore a dark navy tailored suit for the occasion.

"Look at all these people. I didn't think there'd be so many," Judith said, looking amazed.

"I know. Justin's done a tremendous job," smiled Luna as she moved between the guests.

Edward walked over to Justin as he spoke to members of the press and tapped him on the shoulder. Justin turned around in excitement. "You told me this was going to be a small event," said Edward.

"Relax, it's for a good cause and look at the turn out," Justin said, patting him on the back, as they looked on while everyone took their seats for the event. "Are you ready?" Edward nodded.

Justin went up to the stand, and clapped. Everyone in the room fell silent and the last couple of guests sat in their seats.

"Thank you, I just want to say a huge thank you to my team at the paper for organising this event. Dr Edward Sampson has been a big influence across many universities and colleges around the UK. With his debut fiction book, I would like to introduce him to you now… Dr Edward Sampson." A roar of thunderous applause filled the room and everyone clapped. Edward walked onto the makeshift stage.

"Thank you, thank you, Justin. I don't know what to say other than I'm very grateful to be here today to be presenting my new book to you. I could not have done this without the support from my friends, family and colleagues." He paused.

Everyone in the room clapped and cheered as cameras flashed. Luna brought the book onto the stage and handed it to him, kissed him on the cheek, and walked back to where both Judith and Justin stood. They egged him on, giving him the thumbs up. Luna raised her glass to him. Edward tried to keep a serious expression, despite knowing Luna was ready to have a good time.

He looked at the eager guests, smiled, and raised his book in the air. "Thank you, ladies and gentlemen, for coming here today. My name is Dr Edward Sampson, a curator at the London Museum." He paused and stroked his neatly trimmed brown beard. "This is my first work of fiction, created from vast knowledge and professional interest in my specialist and life-long study of local history. The book is called *The Unwanted*. I am happy and honoured to give you a short reading."

Edward opened the book to the first page.

"Howling cries afar,
Haunting footsteps pitter-patter,
Beware of the teeth that chatter,
Striking, biting, clawing, shatter."

•

It was 2pm and Edward chatted away to his fans, and the many press representatives from across the whole country. He shook hands and mingled with as many of his guests as possible.

His phone momentarily interrupted his enjoyment. "Hello," he said, searching for a quiet spot to listen to the caller.

"There you are," Judith said as they came face to face in the roof garden.

"It's freezing," he said, putting the phone into the back pocket of his dark jeans.

"I'll warm you up," she said, snuggling into him, hugging him. She looked into his eyes and kissed him.

"What's that for?" he said, blushing.

"Can't I kiss the man of my life?"

He scooped her up, kissed her back, and in the background, Luna and Justin cheered them on as they ogled from the doorway.

ABOUT THE AUTHOR

Marios Eracleous started writing at the age of sixteen. At school, his teacher asked him to write stories to help him with his English and since then he has been writing and creating web serials for the internet.

His first published work was with Sixth Element Publishing called Harvey Duckman presents, where his stories featured in Harvey Duckman Volumes 1, 3 and the Christmas Special, which can be found on Amazon in paperback and eBook for Kindle.

Marios has written another three short stories in a series called Unexplained Anomalies Terror of the underground, Taste of Blood and the Haematomorph Invasion. A new story is coming soon.

The Unwanted Guests is a standalone book and is available or as an eBook kindle download and in paperback.

Marios enjoys watching a variety of television shows and is a big fan of Doctor Who and loves sci fi and mystery shows especially from 60s, 70s and 80s.

Marios also enjoys going to comic cons such as MCM and London Film Comic Con.

Printed in Great Britain
by Amazon